This book belongs to

★ ───────────────────────────────────── ★

© 2002 by Parragon Books Ltd

This 2006 edition published by Backpack Books by arrangement with Parragon Publishing.

2006 Backpack books

ISBN-13: 978-0-7607-6516-6
ISBN-10: 0-7607-6516-2

Printed and bound in China

3 5 7 9 10 8 6 4

Twinkle
the
TOOTH FAIRY

Written by Nick Ellsworth ★ Illustrated by Michelle White

BACKPACKBOOKS

NEW YORK

Twinkle the Tooth Fairy says…

Look after your baby teeth. Brush them in the morning and before you go to bed. If you have the chance, brush your teeth after meals, too.

Brush round and round, and inside and out.

When one of your baby teeth starts to wobble, it's getting ready to come out. Once it has fallen out, save it for me! Put it in your special tooth purse under your pillow, so that it's easy for me to find.

While you are asleep, I will leave a coin in its place for you to find in the morning!

In time, another tooth will grow to replace your baby tooth. Remember to brush your new teeth carefully too.

Twinkle
x

Twinkle the Tooth Fairy was always very busy. Every night, she collected the baby teeth that the children left under their pillows. But the teeth were so tiny that they were difficult to find in the dark.

Late one summer evening, she was looking for the last baby tooth.

"It must be here somewhere," she thought, tiptoeing around the edge of the bed.

Suddenly, she saw something sparkle in the moonlight. The tiny tooth had fallen on the floor! She picked it up carefully, and put her last shiny coin under the pillow.

"Good night," whispered Twinkle as she gently kissed the sleeping child and flew silently out the window.

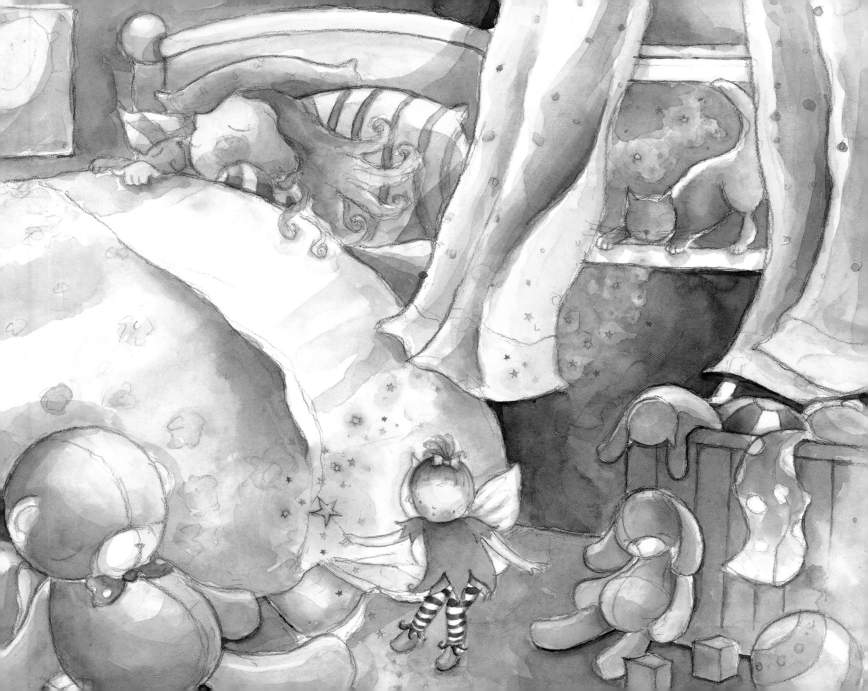

The sun was just coming up as Twinkle flew back to Fairyland.
All the fairies were very busy getting ready for the Fairy Ball.

Fairy food had
to be made
by the best
fairy cooks.

Hundreds of
fairy lights
had to be put up.

And the fairy
orchestra was
practicing very
hard to make
this the best
Fairy Ball ever.

Before going to bed, Twinkle decided to go and see her friend Thimble, the fairy dressmaker. Thimble had been busy too, making all the dresses for the Fairy Ball.

"What beautiful dresses!" exclaimed Twinkle.

"I'm glad you like them," said Thimble. "But they would be so much better if I could decorate them with golden thread. I can't find any in all of Fairyland."

"I know where there's lots of golden thread. Leave it to me!" Twinkle said excitedly, and flew off high into the sky.

She flew higher and higher. Soon she was among hundreds of bright, shining stars. On she flew, until she reached a huge golden ball—the sun. "Please, Sun," she said, "can you spare some of your fine golden thread for my friend Thimble? She needs it to make her dresses for the Fairy Ball."

Twinkle waited. All of a sudden, a long trail of golden thread came
slowly from the center of the sun. Twinkle took the end of it,
and began to pull it toward her.
"Ooh, that tickles," laughed the sun.
Soon Twinkle had gathered a large bundle of the precious thread.

"Thank you, Sun. Your thread will make my friend Thimble very happy."
"You're very welcome, Twinkle," chuckled the sun.
Then Twinkle flew back to Fairyland, being very careful not to drop
the golden thread on the way.

When Thimble saw what Twinkle had brought her, she clapped her hands with joy!

"Thank you, Twinkle. Now my dresses will look perfect! And you will wear the finest one at the Fairy Ball."

"I've never been to the Fairy Ball," said Twinkle quietly.

"Why ever not?" asked Thimble.

"It takes me such a long time to find all the children's teeth, I never get back in time," she said sadly.

"Don't you worry. I'll think of something!" said Thimble. Twinkle felt tired after her busy night and went right to bed.

When Twinkle woke up the next day, she was surprised to see a large bag at the foot of her bed. Inside the bag were the most beautiful purple and gold velvet pouches.

"I wonder what these are for," she thought. Pinned to the bag was a note, which read...

Dear Twinkle,

I have made these special pouches from the leftover fairy dress cloth. The children can put their teeth into them. The pouches will be much easier for you to find in the dark. With a little luck, you will be back in time for the Ball!

Your best fairy friend,

Thimble
x

Later that evening, Twinkle
collected all the children's
baby teeth as usual.
She left each child with a
shiny coin tucked into one
of the pouches, which she
carefully placed under their
pillows. She whispered to
each sleeping child,
"Please use your new pouch
to keep your next baby tooth
safe under your pillow."
When she had finished her
night's work, she flew back
home to sleep.

The night of the Fairy Ball had arrived at last! Everyone had
traveled far and wide to be there.

Twinkle was very excited,
and hoped that she'd be back in time to join in the fun.
But first she had her important job to do.

When she flew off that night to collect the baby
teeth, Twinkle was overjoyed to see that each
child had put their baby tooth inside
the pouch. Now, they were easy to find!

She kissed each
child and whispered,
"Thank you!"

After gathering them all up
carefully, Twinkle flew quickly
back to Fairyland.

When she was almost
home, Twinkle could
hear the sounds of
the fairy orchestra in
the distance.
The whole sky was lit
up from the lights of
the Fairy Ball.
"Oh no! It's already
begun," she thought.
So she flew even
faster.

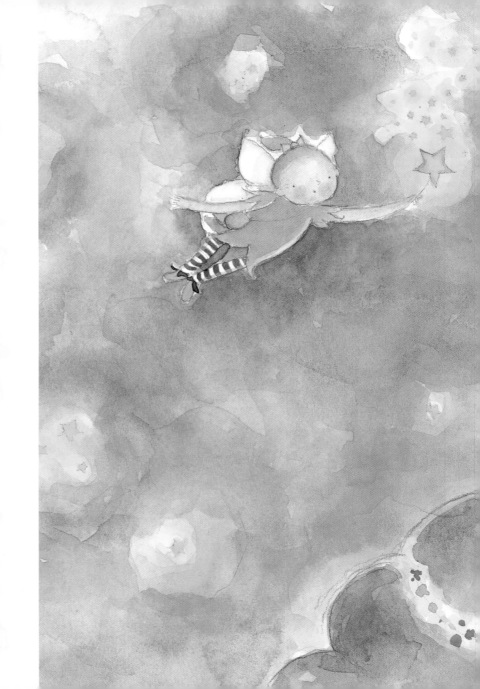

When she reached home, Twinkle rushed to see her friend Thimble.

"Am I too late?" she asked breathlessly.

"It's only just begun!" laughed Thimble. "You have plenty of time." Thimble gave Twinkle one of her beautiful dresses to wear.

While she was dressing, Twinkle told Thimble all about the good children putting their baby teeth in their new pouches.

Twinkle had a wonderful time at the Fairy Ball,
and ate the most delicious fairy food she'd ever tasted.

Twinkle danced for
hours, and didn't feel
the least bit tired.
And everyone agreed
that in her beautiful
new dress, she was
the prettiest fairy
of all.